A Solstice with Jacky Waterman

The Watermen Series
(A Short Story)

by

Carmen DeSousa

A Solstice with Jacky Waterman
The Watermen Series
(A Short Story)
Copyright© 2014 by Carmen DeSousa

ISBN: 9798782547714

www.CarmenDeSousaBooks.com

Cover Design: Viola Estrella

A note from the author ...

Dear friend, I wrote *A Solstice with Jacky Waterman* because I love writing short stories in between my larger projects. Although this story is similar to old-fashioned fairy tales, meaning it's a short, boy-meets-girl fantasy, I plan to develop it into a series. That said, this short story will take you less than an hour to read, but I hope Sirena's story will stay with you and that you'll look forward to the next chapter of her life.

For now, Happy Reading! I'll see you in about an hour.

Carmen

Chapter One

Sirena stared at her image in the mirrored wall of her glamorous suite. She'd sold everything she accumulated in the last ten years to come here.

For one last week to be free. To feel the sand beneath her feet, the sun on her face, and the breeze as it brushed against her skin like a lover's kiss.

Not that she'd felt that kind of kiss in a long time, but she remembered what it felt like the first time she had. The first time he'd kissed her. The man she'd once loved. The man she'd moved to the congested streets of New York to be with.

Her father had warned her about men like him, and he'd been right. Merely months after she'd moved to New York, the man she thought had loved her moved to another bustling city and made it clear that she shouldn't follow him.

She could have forced herself on him, but she wouldn't … couldn't. What good would it do to force someone to love you?

Sirena pulled her long blond hair over her shoulder and weaved threads of silver through each strand as she braided her hair. Her father had always liked when she'd done this, said she looked like the princess she was, the queen she would eventually be. But she'd run away from her heritage … out of fear.

"Will that be all, miss?" The young woman whom she'd hired to assist her this week had turned out to be a delightful companion. "I'd be happy to braid your 'air. You 'ave the most beautiful 'air I've ever seen. It be the color of sunshine. What I wouldn't do for your 'air."

Sirena peeked up at the mirror, smiling at the sweet Jamaican woman who'd answered her ad. "On the contrary, Tia, I think your hair is quite beautiful. And I would love to be as tall and strong as you are. Look at me … I barely come up to your shoulders. I'm unable to even carry my own suitcases without your help."

Tia stepped up behind her, her smile broad and white as her image filled the mirror above Sirena's reflection. The two of them were a sight indeed. "I think you're precious, my lady."

"Thank you, Tia. You've been so gracious to me that I wish I could offer you more than a few days of work."

"What you paid me will feed my family for months, so I'm much obliged." Tia worked her slender fingers through the braid, loosening the strands, and then started over from scratch. When she finished, she laid the long woven tress over Sirena's shoulder again, then walked toward the closet.

Tia reached into the closet for the gown Sirena told her she would wear tonight. The organza fabric shimmered as the young woman swept the dress around in a circle, holding the sweetheart neckline to her chest.

The good-natured woman laughed. "Just lookin' at me image in the mirror makes me feel like a princess." The beaded bodice sparkled beneath the vanity lights as Tia held up the mermaid-style dress – as the saleswoman had referred to it – in front of Sirena. "But it be prettier on you, miss."

Tia held open the dress so Sirena could step inside, then smoothed it up over her hips and bust. She zipped up the back and then stepped back as Sirena stared in the mirror again. She did look like a princess.

That time had passed, though. She'd given up her crown. A tear threatened to escape, but she lifted her head and blinked it away. Tia would be hurt if she ruined her makeup.

"Now, turn so that I can look at you," Tia instructed in her charming native tongue.

Sirena turned, then lowered herself into a curtsy since Tia loved to treat her as though she were royalty, even though she'd never breathed a word about her previous life.

"Ahh … lovely indeed. You look like a princess out of all those fairy tales I read to my daughter."

Sirena smiled. "Thank you, Tia. You sure you don't want to come to dinner with me. I could still buy you that dress downstairs."

"Thank you, miss, but I wouldn't know what to do with me-self at some fancy gathering. I'll be fine and dandy in the magnificent suite you paid for."

Understanding, knowing how she felt the first few days in a new land, Sirena nodded. "Please, order anything you want from room service, then. Don't be shy. This week is about us. You and I, we're going to treat ourselves like royalty. Okay? Tomorrow, we'll both visit the spa."

"Ahh … miss, I feel like a queen just stayin' in dis fancy place. Now, off with you before you miss your dinner and all the fetchin' men who'll be there. You might even find you-self a prince."

Sirena laughed. "I don't think so, Tia, but I'll try to enjoy myself anyway."

Tia held up the silver clutch she'd helped Sirena pick out

and the rhinestone-studded sandals with the dangerously high four-and-a-half-inch heels the salesperson had talked her into purchasing. "Be careful wearin' dese, miss. You don't want to be breakin' you ankle."

With one hand on Tia's shoulder for support, Sirena slipped into the sleek satin shoes and pulled up the tiny zippers at the back of the heels.

She released a long breath as Tia escorted her to the door. "I'll see you in the morning, Tia."

"If you find an 'andsome man. Don't be worryin' about me none. I can keep me-self plenty busy in such a spectacular place."

"That's not going to happen, my friend, but thank you. I'll see you at nine a.m."

Chapter Two

J.W. finished tying his bowtie, then left his hotel room for the restaurant downstairs.

Tonight was the night. He was certain. He'd waited six months for this night, and now he'd be rewarded when he found and returned the princess to her rightful place.

He couldn't be sure, of course, but Fisher Island was the closest place to her destination, and she had to return during the Winter Solstice, the longest night in the Northern Hemisphere.

And he would be here to meet her.

"Good evening, sir. Will you be dining alone again tonight?" The host greeted him in the normal self-important but pleasant fashion that most men in his position radiated. As though serving the rich and famous made them prominent, too.

His back ramrod straight, his chin held firm, J.W. answered with an equal amount of pretension, knowing the man would probably question his standing if he acted any other way. "I am."

J.W. knew that air of importance all too well. He'd worked with many of their kind. He, on the other hand, didn't serve royalty; he was a hunter. Kings hired him when they wanted – rather, needed – his expertise.

The king had dispatched him six months ago, but he

hadn't had any luck. Tonight, his luck would change. He felt it in an almost palpable way. The heavy, humid air had an electric charge to it; he could literally feel the tingle on his tongue, the way he did when the pressure changed in the atmosphere because of an impending storm.

As he'd done the previous nights, he requested a table by the open doors that led out to the pool area and beaches. The dark burgundy walls and gold curtains framed the violet sky beyond the hotel. The resort was magnificent and quiet. The only way to reach the private island was via ferry, so the hustle and bustle of South Beach felt as though it were another world.

Earlier, he'd used the golf cart the concierge had provided him to search the tiny island, looking for the best place for her to depart. The marina most certainly would have a moonlight cruise on the night of the Winter Solstice, so he'd be waiting. If, however, he was lucky enough to find her beforehand, that would be even better.

If he didn't find her, he would just have to wait out his time. Miami wasn't so bad. It'd been hot in the summer, but the breeze off the ocean and the endless sun-bronzed women had made living there for the last six months almost bearable. Still, he wanted to go home, and he couldn't go home without the princess.

J.W. sipped on his mojito, another reward of living in Miami. The smooth white rum, blended with real sugar cane, according to the bartender he'd befriended this afternoon, also had a hint of lime juice, sparkling water, and mint. The traditional Cuban cocktail went down as smoothly as a breath of fresh air, then left a warm sensation flowing through his body that he'd come to enjoy. He never over-indulged, though, as he had to keep his mind sharp. He couldn't take the chance that he would miss the princess.

The scent of salt air drifted through the restaurant, making his mouth water. Then a crash of water from a rogue wave hit the sand. It'd been so calm only minutes earlier, but again, it was that electricity in the air, he assumed.

Elegant palm fronds garlanded with twinkling white lights for Christmas rustled in the wind, pattering against each other as though trying to escape the limbs that contained them. And although white sand, not snow, covered the ground outside, green wreaths decorated with pinecones and holly hung over archways, and evergreen fir trees adorned with silver and blue bulbs festooned every alcove of the resort.

"Just me, sir," a singsong voice captured J.W.'s attention from the symphony of sounds and sights outside the French doors of the dining room.

Petite with delicate features and golden skin that nearly matched her long braided hair, the woman was lovely. Her sapphire eyes met his and, for a moment, he was certain that his heart had stopped beating. Per the woman's instruction, the host escorted her to a table and started to clear the second setting.

J.W. knew he shouldn't … he didn't have time to waste, but he couldn't stop himself. He picked up his drink and strolled toward her.

Two feet from her table, he halted his approach and gestured to the empty seat. "May I?"

"I …" She looked up at the host, who'd halted his clearing of the second seating arrangement. "I suppose."

The host neither smiled nor frowned; he just replaced the items, then waved his hand at a busboy to clean the table J.W. had just exited.

Without hesitation, J.W. pulled out the chair and sat.

"Thank you. I couldn't help but overhear you were dining alone, and it just didn't make sense to me that we should take up two of the best tables in the restaurant."

"I agree. I'm Sirena."

Since she didn't extend her hand, J.W. offered her a slight dip of his head. *Sirena* … She wouldn't go by her real name, of course, but could she be the princess? She couldn't be. Rarely were princesses beautiful, and this woman was the most attractive woman he'd ever seen. At home or here in Florida.

He'd assumed he would know her the moment he saw her. He'd never been wrong before, but now … he wasn't sure. How would he know? He couldn't just ask her. She'd never tell him the truth. She'd run … and with good reason.

"It's my pleasure to meet you, Sirena. I'm J.W."

Chapter Three

Sirena stared at the dark-haired man who'd just made himself comfortable at her table. Something struck her as familiar about the handsome gentleman, but she couldn't quite put her finger on it.

Maybe it was the crackling sensation that seemed to be working its way through her body from the moment she'd stepped inside the restaurant.

The sizzling of her blood had seemed to increase the moment he'd shown up at the foot of her table. Of course, it didn't matter. She had no interest in any man. She'd be leaving in a few days.

"What brings you to Fisher Island?" the man asked as he lifted a small goblet to his lips, but then held back before taking a sip. "Not many single women come to this resort, as it's usually more for honeymooners and families."

"And yet, it appears you're here alone, too," she said in a soft retort.

He lifted his glass as if in a toast, then went to take a sip, but stopped again. "Where are my manners?"

His eyes darted around the room. When he caught the attention of a waiter, he held up his glass, then raised two of his fingers. He turned his eyes back to her, and she couldn't help but smile at his sudden erratic behavior after he'd approached the table with such an air about him.

She couldn't help but stare at the unique shade of his blue eyes, like no other color she'd ever seen. She searched for the right word to describe the deepest blue of the nighttime sky before it turned black. Indigo, she decided. His eyes looked like a dark purplish blue.

The man swirled the liquid in front of him. "Do you like mojitos?"

"I've never tried one."

"Really? They're quite delicious."

She peeked up as the waiter approached with two drinks. "Well, I guess I'll get my chance soon enough."

J.W. set his glass that still had a few ounces in it on the tray, then reached for his new glass, holding it up again. "To the only single people on Fisher Island."

Sirena lifted her glass as well, not sure why she was toasting to his proclamation, certain it wasn't true anyway. "Or at least the only two in here," she offered.

"That works." He clinked his glass to hers, then finally took a long pull off his cocktail. "Ahh ..."

She took a sip, then nodded. "It's tasty. Refreshing."

"It is. So, back to my first question. What brings you here?"

"The sun," she answered easily. "I've been in New York for the last ten years, so I thought it would be nice to soak up the sun over the holidays. And you?"

"I live here. I have a condo in South Beach, but it's ... busy. It's nice to get away from all the hustle and bustle for a few days." He paused only a second and then shot another question at her. "What do you do for a living?"

"Are we playing twenty questions, J.W.?"

He shrugged. "Just curious. Isn't that how people get to know each other?"

Sirena resisted a sigh but couldn't contain a half-chuckle,

half-huff from leaving her lips. "I suppose."

"Do you know of a better way?"

"No … it's just … Well, I'm leaving in a few days, so why should I bother to get to know anyone?"

He tilted his head and stared at her with those midnight-blue eyes. "You want me to leave, then?"

She bit her lip and shook her head. "Company would be nice." Other than Tia, she hadn't allowed anyone to get close enough to ask her to dinner … or what she did for a living. She hadn't felt the need since she knew she'd be leaving soon.

The waiter approached, halting their conversation. After they'd ordered the almost identical plate of salad and sushi, they both gazed, as if in longing, at the dark water beyond the array of palm trees.

"Since you won't tell me, let me guess," J.W. started speaking without warning her, his eyes still set on the outside scenery. "A model."

She laughed. "That's not very original, J.W. And here I thought you were some sort of smooth Casanova."

He turned back to her, a small smile playing on his lips. "Not just any model. You model for fairy-tale princess dolls, but you make sure that the image is pure and realistic, so little girls can dream of more than just knights in shining armor and glamorous castles."

Sirena covered her mouth to hold back a laugh … or maybe it was a gasp, since he was so close to how she felt about the false expectations of being a princess. "You're close with the image part, but you're way off everywhere else. I'm a graphic designer."

"Can I see some of your designs? I bet you I'm not that far off."

She closed her eyes and released a sigh this time. "I didn't bring my portfolio. I didn't know I would be at an interview over dinner."

"I'm sure you have an iPhone. You could show me there."

Sirena picked up her fork and took a bite of her salad. "You're wrong again. I don't have a cell phone. You could look on yours."

"I don't have a phone either, but I thought I was the last person in the world to refuse to carry one."

Following her lead, he picked up his fork, too. He really was a gentleman. He'd refused to drink before her and hadn't touched his food until she did, she noticed. Almost as though he'd been accustomed to dining with royalty.

J.W. couldn't know who she was, could he?

Chapter Four

After dinner, J.W. escorted Sirena out to the patio. Once again, the cool but slightly humid Florida air around him seemed to crackle with excitement.

His arm resting on the small of her back, he directed her to the boardwalk. "Would you like to take a walk on the beach?"

She looked down at her shoes. "In these. I don't think I could manage."

"We could walk barefoot. It's an upscale resort. I don't think anyone will run off with our shoes."

"Okay …" she said, and if he weren't mistaken, he'd swear she sounded downright giddy at the notion.

He kicked off his shoes and pulled off his socks, then hid both pairs of shoes beneath a vacant lounge chair. He peered around the patio area, at a few hotel guests who still occupied chairs around the pool, even though the sun had sunk behind the hotel hours ago. Several people even swam in the chlorine-tainted pool, which he'd noticed earlier wasn't heated. He preferred the tropical temperature and salty water of the Atlantic.

J.W. offered Sirena his elbow, knowing that if he were wrong, and she wasn't the princess, he was making a grave mistake, one that would cost him the next ten years of his life.

At the moment, though, that didn't matter to him. If he was wrong and she was just a beautiful woman from New York, who wanted to escape her life for a few days, maybe he could convince her to stay a little longer. He might not miss home so much with her on his arm.

He stared down at her from his six-foot frame. She barely reached his shoulders without her heels. "So are you originally from New York? You don't have an accent."

"I moved to New York with a man I fell in love with years ago."

"Oh," he said, not sure where to go from there. He'd hoped he could decipher more of her answers to prove that she was the princess. Her answer, however, sent his mind in a different direction. "Are you still in love with the man?"

"It's been over between us for years."

Her voice sounded sad, distant. What man would leave such a beautiful, sweet woman? Of course, he'd only met her hours earlier, but he'd learned to trust his judgment. Most people were easy to read. If they were unkind, selfish, or arrogant, it wasn't hard to pick out those qualities within minutes.

He stepped off the boardwalk and extended his hand. Her creamy, soft skin felt warm in his palm. "I can't say that disappoints me," he said, wondering how he could force his mind back to the questions that his duty demanded he ask. At the moment, he only wanted to know how to make this lovely woman his forever.

Sirena stopped walking, so he turned to her. She hadn't released his hand, and she wasn't staring at him. Instead, she dug her toes in the cool grains of the moist sand.

Without warning, a smile lifted his cheek. "What are you doing?"

She shrugged. "It feels good. I haven't done this in years."

He dug his toes into the sand, too. It did feel good. He removed his jacket and spread it out on the sand. He lowered her to the makeshift beach blanket, then slid down beside her. "I hope you don't mind sharing. I didn't bring two jackets, and I didn't know I'd be walking on the beach or I would have brought a towel."

"I don't mind."

The jacket wasn't quite wide enough with their shoulders touching, so he wrapped his arm around her. Suddenly, he felt like a young lad out on his first date.

"J.W., why are you really here?" she asked without looking at him, her eyes set on the ocean that had suddenly crept up to meet them. Each wave seemed to crash a fraction closer than the last as if wanting to pull them both out to sea.

"I told you. For peace and quiet."

"Please don't lie to me."

He cupped her face with his hand, urging her to look at him. "I can't go home without you."

She sighed. "That's what I thought. Who sent you?"

"Your father."

Sirena inhaled a deep breath. "Why? I would have thought – hoped – that they wouldn't think I was ever coming back."

"You're to be married –"

She pulled back. "But I … I can't. I thought –"

"He won't accept anyone but you, Sirena, and now I know why." J.W. struggled with what he wanted to do. If he kissed her, the king – or the prince – might kill him. He wanted to. He couldn't, though. He had to do his job … he had to protect the realm.

"I don't love him. I could never love him. Isn't there anyone else?"

J.W. shook his head. "He'll only accept you. He gave your father until the ten-year mark for your return. If you don't return –"

"My father will no longer be king," Sirena finished his sentence, dropping her head into her hands. "I can't marry him. He's … he's evil."

He tilted his head. He understood her not wanting to marry the prince. But evil? "What do you mean?"

As if not wanting to talk about it, she shook her head. "What if I was dead? How would they know?"

He narrowed his eyes. "What are you saying, Sirena?"

"I could take you back, then I'll –"

"No!" He pulled her toward him. "No … I couldn't let you."

Not caring about the consequences, he folded his arms around her. She didn't fight him, so he dropped his chin and touched his lips to hers. Sweet and salty, like the ocean itself. He took her top lip, her bottom lip, then slid his tongue inside her luscious mouth, relishing the heat and the flavor of her kiss. She opened up to him, and he knew he could never let her go back to the prince.

Sirena pulled back after a few seconds, her face flushed. "Oh, wow … That feels so good, but I can't do this. You're right, though. I can't just kill myself or disappear. That wouldn't solve anything."

He shook his head. "No, it won't."

"I just assumed he would move on to another kingdom, another princess … If he hasn't moved on, the deal will be broken, and he'll become king by default. I can't allow that. My father's kingdom is the largest. If he's allowed to rule –"

"What are you afraid of, Sirena?"

"The prince confided in me. Before our wedding. He said that when our two kingdoms joined, he would have enough soldiers to take over all the realms. Then, he'll kill anyone who won't join him."

Chapter Five

Not sure what she could do or where she could go other than home, Sirena jumped up from the sand, then ran toward the boardwalk. She wanted to flee, but there was no longer an escape for her. Not here, not home.

If she went home, her father would force her to marry the prince, and then that evil man will become the most powerful king the world has ever known. If she didn't go home, the prince would become king anyway, though.

"Sirena, wait!" J.W. called behind her. He caught up with her and touched her shoulder. "Let me help."

"You can't help me," she sneered. "You came here so you could deliver me to him."

"I came here for your father. Maybe he knows something we don't."

She dropped her head against his chest. She couldn't be mad at J.W. How could he have known? How could anyone have known what the prince had planned? Their world had been peaceful for thousands of years. Her people had all but eradicated war after their kind had almost gone extinct … because of pettiness. Over what? Different thoughts, beliefs, preferences. What difference did their ideals make if they were all dead?

"Trust me, Sirena. Trust your father. He sent me to bring

you back to him. Maybe he knows the prince's heart and has a plan. Why else would he have sent me?"

Sirena looked up at him. "What does J.W. mean?"

He shook his head. "Why do you ask?" Her question had clearly thrown him. Had he been playing a game? Had she told him too much and he'd just been playing along? Did he really know who – what – she was?

"I need to know you are real."

"My name is as real as yours, Siren … Not very discreet."

She sighed. "I guess I'm not that clever. And J.W.?"

"Jacky Waterman."

Sirena covered her mouth to hold back her giggle. "No one questions a Jacky, huh?"

"Not when you have gold, they don't." He pulled her back into his arms. "You don't know me, Sirena. I may not be a prince, but I have an army at my disposal, too. Like our ancestors, my family will never allow a war to happen again so we will take out a threat before it grows into something larger. Maybe that's why your father sought me out."

"But why does he need me?"

"Maybe he wants you to marry someone else?"

She frowned up at him. "Another prince? I'd rather not."

"Who says you have to marry a prince? What if you married someone from another realm, though … a realm without princes?" J.W. dropped to his knee. "What if you married me?"

"You don't even know me … I don't know you."

He smiled. "We'll make it a long engagement. I'll save your kingdom, preserve our way of life, and then you'll happily fall into my arms as my bride."

"You know, Jacky Waterman, I can almost picture that happening."

He stood back up and pulled her into his arms. The man

she'd only known but a few hours, and yet it felt like she'd known her entire life, planted another mind-blowing kiss on her. Maybe her father *had* sent him. Maybe he'd given her time to find herself, knowing she would want to do what was right and save her kingdom.

Chapter Six

Sirena kissed Tia on the cheek and then moved to get out of the limousine she'd rented to drop her off at the marina and then take Tia to her home.

"Miss, you sure you won't be needing the car after the boat ride?"

"No, Tia. I won't be coming back for a long time."

"Wha'cha mean, miss? The boat comes back here, no?"

"I'm going home, Tia." Sirena opened her tiny clutch that held the last of her money. It was enough to pay Tia's bills for a year anyway. Maybe she'd be able to move to a safer neighborhood.

Tia pushed the purse back to her. "No, miss. I can't."

"Tia …" Sirena sung softly, staring into her eyes. She rarely used her gift, but sometimes, if she used it for the good, she would. Her ancestors had used it for war; she only used it for love. "Take it. I'll see you again someday."

The Jamaican lady clutched the purse to her chest as tears sprang to her eyes. "You're … you're magical."

"Something like that." Sirena smiled as she opened the door. "Be well, my friend." The woman just smiled back this time, so she shut the door and walked toward the dock.

Jacky Waterman stood next to the boat that would take them to their ocean current ten miles off shore. He looked striking in his black tuxedo that matched her sleek black satin dress.

He held out his hand. "Shall we?"

For the first time in years, she wasn't afraid. She wasn't fearful of what life held for her or if she'd ever feel loved again. She felt it all. The last three days with Jacky had proven to be the most wonderful days of her life.

They couldn't stay until Christmas, they had to leave during the Winter Solstice, and so Jacky had offered her Christmas gift to her early. She stared down at the fabulous diamond ring on her left hand. The prince would be angry when they arrived, but then, he'd probably show his true colors, then Jacky and she would fight for their home together.

As the sun dipped below the horizon in the west, the boat set sail east, toward the Gulf Stream. Within minutes of casting off, waiters passed around flutes of champagne.

"Merry Christmas, Sirena," Jacky said, holding up his glass.

She tapped her flute to his. "Merry Christmas, Jacky Waterman. I wish I could have shown you snow. There aren't too many things as beautiful as a white Christmas."

"Maybe we'll come back on our tenth anniversary," he offered, placing a warm kiss on her cheek.

"And have to spend ten more years here. I don't think so. I'm sure we can find someplace uninhabited in the Artic to sneak a peek."

He smiled. "I've created a rebel. First the prince, and now you want to break one of our laws."

Sirena nuzzled her head against his shoulder. "Maybe it's time humans started believing in magic again."

She turned and looked back at the other passengers, who, as she suspected, were congregating around the front of the boat.

The sun had completely disappeared, leaving only a hint of pink in the west. At the same time, the full moon breached silvery over the east, as if lighting their way.

Jacky reached for her hand. "Ready, my love?"

Sirena set down her glass and accepted his hand. He helped her up to the back of the boat and then stepped up beside her.

Without a second of indecision, they dove into the sea. Within seconds, they shed their clothes, and their skin transformed. Hers, her normal silver with shades of purple and mauve. Jacky's skin turned into a beautiful array of gold and onyx that shimmered in the crystal blue water.

She turned and kissed Jacky, then took his hand.

With a swish of their fins, they pushed deeper and deeper, letting the Gulf Stream transport them to her kingdom under the sea.

And they lived …

Well, let's see …

Here's a quick blurb of The Watermen Series.

On land, the watermen had never been much different from humans. In fact, other than the subliminal power of their divine voices, their strength was comparable. In the water, though, a waterman was superior.

After the continents split and fathoms of water had separated the two species, humans forgot the magic of the watermen, and later, feared them for their differences. When humankind's fear drove humans to hunt the peaceful race, the watermen's song became their weapon, and soon, humans became the hunted.

Not all watermen agreed with this practice, and war ensued, diminishing the numbers of the once great race. Fearing extinction, the Great King brought all the realms together, decreeing policies forbidding war and limiting interaction with humans. If a waterman desired to visit the surface, he or she had to remain on land until the tenth solstice.

Now, one waterman prince wants to dominate the sea again and eventually, the land, and only Sirena, the princess he's supposed to marry, can stop him.

If you enjoyed *A Solstice with Jacky Waterman*, please consider telling others what you thought on Amazon.com, Goodreads.com, and/or BookBub.com. It doesn't have to be fancy, just a few words to let other readers know if they should download it, too. It means so much to an author to hear what readers loved about a book, and it's much appreciated!

Thank you!

Carmen

A follow-up note ...

So, it has been less than an hour, and as promised, I said we'd talk again. As a child, I loved reading fairy tales. Remember those little tidbits? They weren't long, but they were to the point. Girl has a problem, girl runs. Boy meets girl, and suddenly, her problem is his. Then all works out, and they live happily ever after.

I like to take my stories a little further, and I like to write them for the young at heart, not just for the youngsters. Why can't we as adults still believe in a little magic? And ... what if all the stories we've heard over our lifetime were based on a modicum of truth? To me, it only makes sense that these stories came about for a reason. So, I take on the myths, do tons of research, and see if I can make sense of them all. While I'm researching the rest of Sirena's "tale," please take a look at some of my other stories based on myths. My hope is that when you read, you'll say, "Hmm ... what if?"

The Creatus Series

For four thousand years, creatus have concealed themselves from the humans who hunted them almost to extinction. Now, one creatus will endanger them all by breaking one of their laws: falling in love--with a human.

The Creatus series is not your normal paranormal story … it's a realistic romantic mystery based on the myths you've heard your entire life. Prepare to believe.

Creatus Series
Creatus (They Exist)
Creatus
Creatus Rogue
Creatus Eidolon
Creatus Animus
Creatus Talis

Find links to the Creatus series on my website: www.CarmenDeSousaBooks.com

American Haunts Collection
The Pit Stop (This Stop Could be Life or Death)
The Depot (When Life and Death Cross Tracks)
The Library (Where Life Checks Out)

Find links to all my mysteries with a paranormal edge www.CarmenDeSousaBooks.com/American-Haunts!

Although all of my stories have a common thread — romance and suspense — not all my stories have supernatural elements. If you haven't read any of my romantic suspense books, please check them out. No supernatural abilities, but I'd like to believe the characters in my series are still heroes.

The Midnight Sons
Sam's Folly
Alex's Atonement
Vince's Chance
Erik's Revelation

You can find all my books on my website,
www.CarmenDeSousaBooks.com.

People often ask ... where is that place located that you wrote about? Well, sometimes I make up a restaurant or a building, but other times it is a place I've visited ... or a combination of places. Sometimes, I'll use the outside of one place, and the inside of another place, no different from what they do in the movies.

But ... if it's somewhere you can visit, I've started putting together a Pinterest Page. You can find my Pinterest Pages at www.pinterest.com/Carmen_DeSousa.